I WAS BORN TO BE A SISTER

I Was Born

to Be a
Sister

By Akaela S. Michels-Gualtieri

Illustrated by Marcy Dunn Ramsey

Platypus Media, LLC
Washington DC USA

Available in this series:
I WAS BORN TO BE A BROTHER, with story and music CD, by Zaydek G. Michels-Gualtieri
I WAS BORN TO BE A SISTER, with story and music CD, by Akaela S. Michels-Gualtieri

Activity Guide available at PlatypusMedia.com

The Library of Congress has cataloged the previous edition as follows:
Library of Congress Cataloging-in-Publication Data

Michels-Gualtieri, Akaela S.,
    I was born to be a sister / by Akaela S. Michels-Gualtieri; illustrated by
Marcy Dunn Ramsey.
        p. cm.
Summary: A girl who felt born to be a sister wants to send her baby
brother back after he screams during her birthday party, knocks down her
cheese tower, and other baby behavior.
[1. Babies--Fiction. 2. Sisters--Fiction. 3. Brothers and
sisters--Fiction. 4. Sibling rivalry--Fiction.] I. Ramsey, Marcy Dunn,
ill. II. Title
    ISBN 1-930775-03-2 (alk. paper)
    PZ7.M5817 Iae 2001
    [E]--dc21

                                                            2001000615

I WAS BORN TO BE A SISTER, with story and music CD, ISBN: 1-930775-11-3
Copyright © 2003 Platypus Media, LLC
First printing 2001

10 9 8 7 6 5 4 3 2

Platypus Media is committed to the promotion and protection of breastfeeding.
We donate six percent of our profits to breastfeeding organizations.

Platypus Media, LLC
627 A Street, NE
Washington, DC 20002
PlatypusMedia.com

Editor: Ellen E.M. Roberts, Where Books Begin, New York, NY
Designer: Douglas Wink, Inkway Graphics, Santa Fe, NM

Manufactured in the United States of America

To Mom and Dad—
who made me a sister!

Some girls were born
to be princesses.

Some were born
to be redheads.

I was born to be a sister.

When I was three, my baby brother was born. I was a sister at last. This was what I was meant to be!

In the beginning, it was so much fun.

I clapped my baby brother's feet together
to make him smile.

I sang "Rock-A-Bye-Baby" to him to make him fall asleep.

I squeezed a sponge
over his belly
to make him clean.

I taught him to slurp his spaghetti at dinnertime.

But after a while, being a sister wasn't so fun anymore.

"Why do I have to be a sister?" I whispered to my mom.

"Can't we send him back?" I asked my dad when my
brother wasn't listening.

My brother splashed water in my face when I was getting ready to do a somersault in the pool.

He crashed
into me
when
I was
doing
cartwheels.

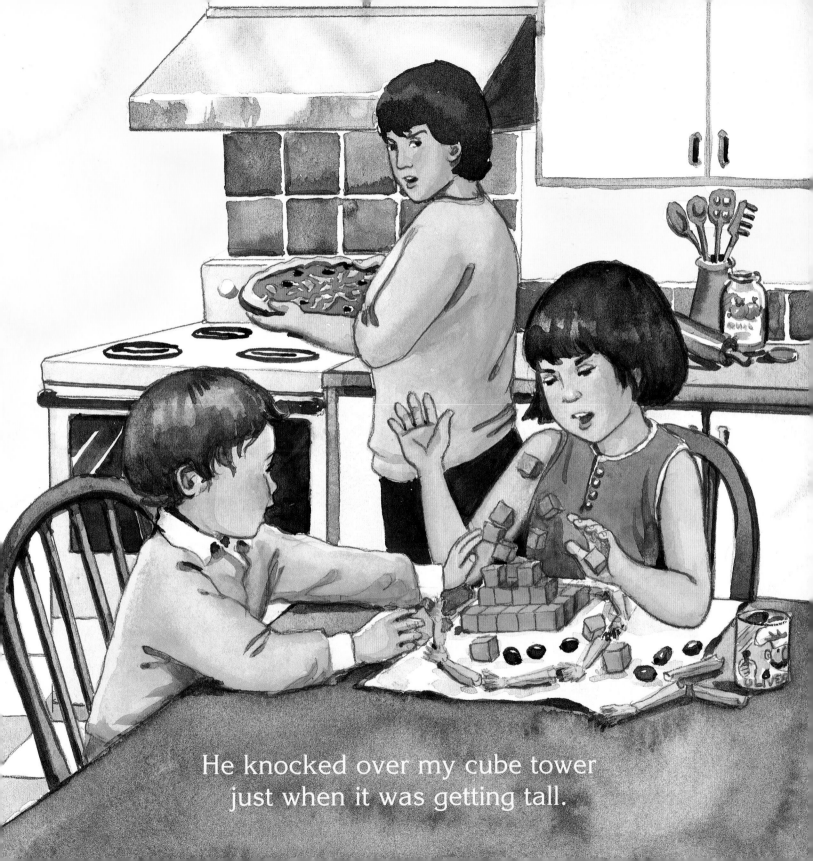

He knocked over my cube tower
just when it was getting tall.

He screamed without stopping while everyone else sang "Happy Birthday" to me at my party.

By the time fall came, I hated being a sister.

"Maybe he can move into his own apartment,"
I told Mom.

"Maybe we'll lose him at the mall," I told Dad.

The best part of starting school was getting away from my baby brother. But when I came home, he was waiting for me.

He wanted to play
castle. I showed him
how to slay a dragon.

Mom made me take him to my school
on Harvest Day. He turned the hose on and off for us
so we could water our marigolds.

He brought all the red candies for me from Jack's birthday party.

Dad says he's learning to share.

Everywhere I go, he's always following me, asking questions and copying what I do. He remembers every word I say and every song I sing. It's a lot of work to be a sister.

It's a big job, but then,
I'm a big sister.

The chorus to the song "I Was Born to Be a Sister"
©2001 Platypus Media, LLC
For full song, visit PlatypusMedia.com
CD with this song and "I Was Born to Be a Brother" available from Platypus Media

Arrangement by Donald Sosin and Joanna Seaton,
Farmhouse Window Productions, Lakeville CT